DISNEY·PIXAR TOY STORY STORYBOOK COLLECTION

Toy Story
Storybook
Collection

Disney · PIXAR

Toy Story
Storybook
Collection

PaRRagon

Bath · New York · Singapore · Hong Kong · Cologne · Delhi · Melbourne

First published by Parragon in 2009
Parragon
Queen Street House
4 Queen Street
Bath BA1 1HE, UK

ISBN 978-1-4075-6036-6
Printed in China

TABLE OF CONTENTS

BUZZ LIGHTYEAR

WOODY

JESSIE

SLINKY

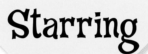

Starring

HAMM

REX

BO PEEP

BULLSEYE

Andy was a very lucky boy. He had lots of different toys. But his favourite toy was a cowboy named Woody.

Andy loved to
play with Woody.

But there was something Andy didn't know about Woody and the other toys. When Andy wasn't around, the toys had a life of their own. They **moved**. They **talked**. They **laughed**. And they had **adventures**.

All toys do. But only when no one is **watching**.

One year, Andy got a brand-new toy for his birthday – a space ranger named **Buzz Lightyear**! Buzz had flashing **lasers, gadgets** and even **wings**.

Buzz thought he was a **real space ranger**. He even thought he could **fly**! Woody tried to tell Buzz that he was actually a toy. But Buzz wouldn't listen.

Soon Buzz became Andy's new favourite toy. This made Woody **sad**.

One day, Andy was going to Pizza Planet. His mum told him he could bring just one toy. Woody wanted to go! He tried to shove Buzz aside. But he accidentally pushed Buzz out of Andy's bedroom **window** instead. **Whoops!**

Woody got to go with Andy, but the other toys were very **upset**. They thought Woody had pushed Buzz on purpose.

Woody felt bad –
until Buzz turned up
in the car, too!

Buzz was **angry** with Woody. The two began to fight. When the car stopped at a gas station, they tumbled out of the back door.

Oh, no! Andy and his mum drove off to Pizza Planet, leaving Buzz and Woody behind. They had become **lost toys!** And Andy's family was moving to a new home in just two days.

Then Woody spotted a **Pizza Planet truck**. Woody told Buzz the truck was a spaceship, and they hopped on board.

Buzz insisted on riding up front. Luckily, a stack of pizza boxes kept him hidden from the driver.

At Pizza Planet, Buzz climbed into a claw game filled with **toy aliens**. Buzz thought the game was a **spaceship**.

Woody tried to get Buzz out – but soon they were both trapped!

Oh, no! Andy's mean neighbour, **Sid**, captured Buzz and Woody. Sid loved to torture toys. Woody and Buzz were in **trouble**! Sid took Buzz and Woody home with him.

Sid's room was full of **mutant toys**. He had created them by combining different toy parts in strange ways . . . and now he had evil plans for Buzz and Woody! They had to escape.

Buzz tried to **fly** out of Sid's house, but he fell. He finally realized that Woody was right – he wasn't a real space ranger. He was only a **toy**.

Sid strapped a **rocket** to Buzz. He planned to blow Buzz to pieces! Buzz and Woody had to work **together** if they were going to escape.

But Buzz didn't want to escape. He felt sad because he wasn't a real space ranger. Woody helped Buzz understand that Andy loved him and that being a **toy** was very important.

And before they knew it, Buzz and Woody had become **friends**.

Woody came up with a plan to save Buzz. He asked **Sid's toys** to help. Just as Sid was about to **blow** Buzz up, Woody and the mutant toys came to life. Sid was **terrified** – he screamed and ran away!

Buzz and Woody were thrilled! So were Sid's toys. They knew that Sid would never torture them again.

Now Buzz and Woody were free to go back to Andy. But Andy's removal van was already pulling away from his house. They had to catch up with it!

Buzz and Woody ran and ran. Sid's mean dog, **Scud**, began to **chase** them!

Luckily, RC came out of the moving van to give Buzz and Woody a ride. They thought they were home free – until RC's batteries began to run down!

Then they remembered that Buzz still had Sid's **rocket** strapped to his back. Woody launched it. Whoosh! Buzz, Woody and RC flew through the air. RC landed safely in the back of the moving van. But Buzz and Woody kept going.

Buzz popped open his **wings**. The rocket flew into the air and exploded.
Buzz and Woody were **falling**! But thanks to Buzz's wings, they were falling
with style. Buzz held on to Woody and veered towards **Andy's car**.

Buzz and Woody glided through the car's **sunroof** and plopped down next to **Andy** – right where they belonged.

Do **you** like toys?

Well, Andy sure does. He has all kinds of toys, and he loves to play with each and every one of them.

37

But Andy's favourite toys are a cowboy named Woody . . .

. . . and a space ranger named Buzz Lightyear!

One day, something terrible happened.

Woody was **toynapped**!

You see, Woody wasn't just a toy.

He was a **FAMOUS** toy who once had his own TV show.

Along with Jessie the cowgirl, Bullseye the horse and Stinky Pete the prospector, Woody starred in *Woody's Roundup*.

Because Woody and the other Roundup toys were so famous, Al, a greedy toy-store owner, was going to sell them to a museum – all the way across the world in **Japan**!

Jessie, Bullseye and the Prospector were very excited. They had been in **STORAGE** for a long time.

But Woody didn't want to go to a silly **museum**! He wanted to go back home to Andy!

That is, he did until Jessie told him a story. Just as Woody had Andy, Jessie once had a little girl who loved her.

They played together.

They laughed together.

They spent every day together – until the
girl grew up and forgot all about Jessie.

DONATIONS

Woody began to wonder if Andy would grow up and forget
about him. Maybe the museum wouldn't be so bad after all. . . .

Meanwhile, Buzz Lightyear had been busy planning a rescue mission.

Slinky Dog,

Hamm,

Buzz

and **Rex**

all set off together to find Woody.

47

To get to Al's Toy Barn, the toys had to cross a busy street.
Fortunately, they had a plan.

Inside the store, Buzz and the others had to face another challenge – a new (and confused) Buzz Lightyear toy.

And little did they know that an evil toy named Emperor Zurg was hot on their trail!

But **nothing** would stop Buzz and his friends from finding Woody!

49

They quickly found Al in the office of the toy store and followed him to his apartment – and there was Woody!

But there was one **problem**.

Woody had decided to go to the museum with the other Roundup toys. He didn't want to end up **forgotten** and in **storage**.

Buzz tried to convince Woody to go home to Andy, but the cowboy had made up his mind. So Buzz and the others left – without Woody.

It didn't take Woody long to realize that he had made a mistake. His true place was with Andy, not in a museum!

But the Prospector had a different plan. He was going to the museum, and no **cowboy** would stand in his way. He trapped Woody, Jessie and Bullseye in the apartment. Then Al took them away.

Woody's friends had to rescue him, but first they had to defeat **Zurg**!

Now they had to hurry – Al was on his way to the airport. Next stop, **Japan**!

Buzz Lightyear to the **rescue**!

Buzz, Hamm, Rex and Slinky borrowed a car and raced to the airport.

54

They rescued Woody
and Bullseye –
and sent the
Prospector packing!

Unfortunately,
poor Jessie got
stuck on the plane!

Would Woody and Buzz be able to save her?

Of course they would!

Soon Woody, Buzz, Rex, Hamm and Slinky were back in Andy's room – along with their new friends, Jessie and Bullseye!

All the toys knew they couldn't stop Andy from growing up – but they wouldn't miss it for the world!

WELCOME home ANDY

BUZZ'S BIG MISSION

Buzz Lightyear the space ranger stood by Andy's window and looked at the night sky. Stars were twinkling, and the moon was full.

Buzz sighed. Outer space. Once, he thought space was where he had come from. That was before he knew he was a toy. Still, he was an adventurer and had always wanted to explore space. That hadn't changed.

Buzz remembered that Andy had made a wish upon a star once. So Buzz looked for the brightest star in the sky and made his own wish. Then he quietly hopped onto the bed and went to sleep next to Andy.

The next morning, Buzz overheard Andy talking with his mother.

"Mum, I forgot to tell you!" Andy said excitedly. "The science club at school made a spaceship. They're going to launch it in the park tomorrow. They said I could watch it blast off. Can I, Mum, please, can I?"

"Sure," Andy's mum replied.

A spaceship, Buzz thought. Scientists! His wish had come true – this was his chance to explore space. Andy pushed the button on Buzz's back.

"To infinity and beyond!" Buzz exclaimed.

Soon, Andy left for school. The moment the door closed, the toys came to life.

On the bed, Buzz jumped to his feet. "Attention, everyone!" he cried. "I have an announcement. Tomorrow I am going into space – on a spaceship!"

"Ooooh!" Everyone was impressed.

Everyone, that is, except Woody the cowboy, one of Andy's favourite toys.

"Buzz," he said, "remember when Sid strapped you to that rocket and you were almost sent into space? That was really dangerous!"

"This is not a rocket, but an official spaceship created by highly trained scientists," Buzz said. "Now I need to prepare for the mission. You must all help me train!"

"Sure," the toys agreed. "We'll help you, Buzz."

"Phase one, fitness training!" Buzz called to the other toys.

Buzz jumped off the bed. Below him, Hamm the piggy bank nudged a big red rubber ball into place. Buzz landed on the ball and bounced high into the air, exactly as planned. He grabbed a dolls' clothes hanger, which had been hanging on a jump rope that was strung across the room.

Buzz zipped down the jump rope. When he got to the end of it, he leaped to the floor.

From there, he turned and hopped in and out of RC Car's spare tyres, which had been set out below the jump rope. After the tyres, it was time for chin-ups. Rex the dinosaur had rigged a pencil between two towers of blocks. He gave Buzz a lift to the pencil and stepped away. Twenty chin-ups later, Buzz ran for the finish line, which was strung across the closet door. When he reached it, the toys cheered.

"Phase two," Buzz told the toys, "spin training." He stood in front of a clear plastic ball like the ones hamsters roll around in. He climbed in through a small doorway and braced his arms and legs against the sides of the ball. "Okay, RC!" he yelled at the race car. "Give me a push."

RC revved his engine and gave the ball a big push. The ball rolled over and over. Inside it, Buzz turned every which way. He went all around the room. Finally, the ball banged into a wall. The hatch fell open, and Buzz tumbled out.

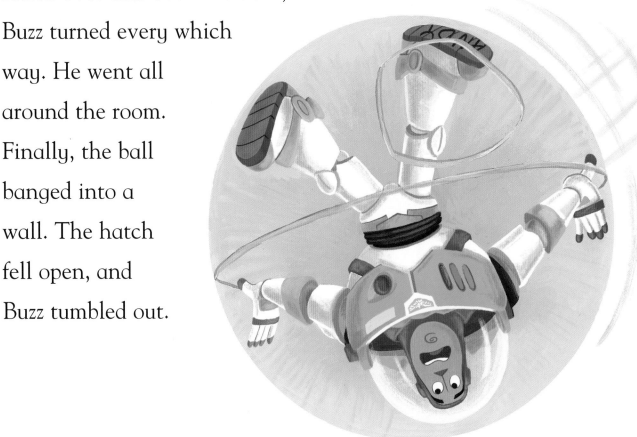

The toys ran over and clustered around him. "Buzz?" said Rex.

"Are you all right, pardner?" Woody asked worriedly.

Buzz unrolled himself. "I am all right!" he cried. "Have no fear!"

The rest of the day was filled with more training. Buzz got language lessons from the little green alien toys. He learned how to say, "Greetings from planet Earth," and, "I come in peace." They also showed him a secret alien handshake.

The Green Army Men taught him some self-defence moves, in case he had to fight space enemies. He even practised his karate chop on the sergeant.

Buzz knew that the temperature changed a lot in space. Once the spaceship left Earth, the air would get really cold. So Buzz stood in front of the air conditioner for an hour to prepare for the cold temperatures.

Then, Bo Peep found a hair dryer and got Rex to hold it. That way, Buzz could feel how warm it would get if the spaceship got close to the sun.

By the end of the day, Buzz felt ready to go to space.

Just before Andy's bedtime, Buzz gathered all the toys. "I'll be back in a few years when I've finished my mission. This is one small step for toys . . . one giant leap for toykind," Buzz said.

Andy will be all grown up by then, thought Woody.

Buzz turned to Bo Peep. "Bye, Bo," he said. "Take care of those sheep. Bye, Rex. Practise your roar every day. Bye, Slinky Dog. Be a good dog. Bye, Hamm. Remember, a penny saved is a penny earned. Bye, Etch A Sketch. Keep drawing."

Etch A Sketch doodled TO INFINITY AND BEYOND on his screen.

Buzz turned to Woody and shook his hand. "Are you sure you want to do this, Buzz?" Woody asked him.

"Of course!" Buzz cried. He put his arm around Woody's shoulders. "Besides, now it will be like it was before I got here."

"You're my friend. I don't want you to go," Woody said sadly. "But I hope you find everything you're searching for."

TO INFINITY
AND BEYOND

That night, when Andy and all the other toys were asleep, Buzz stared out of the window at the moon. Tomorrow, he would be up there.

In the morning, Andy jumped out of bed. "It's launch day!" he shouted. He grabbed Buzz and ran downstairs.

From the window, Woody, Rex, Hamm, Slinky and Bo Peep watched as Andy ran down the street towards the park. He was holding Buzz tightly in his hand. Woody gave Buzz a wave. He thought he saw Buzz wave back.

Half an hour later, the toys saw the spaceship streak up into the sky, before it disappeared behind distant trees. Bo Peep turned away sadly. Slinky buried his head in Woody's side. Woody patted him.

The toys watched out the window for a long time. Finally, Woody whispered, "Goodbye, Buzz."

A while later the toys heard Andy run upstairs and put something by his door before racing away.

"Why's everybody so sad?" a familiar voice asked.

The toys turned and saw Buzz peeking around the door frame.

"Buzz!" Woody cried. "But what about the spaceship? We saw it blast off."

Buzz shrugged. "It looked more like a rickety remote-control aeroplane than a high-tech space vehicle. Besides, I realized something." He lifted up his foot and looked fondly at the bottom of it. ANDY was written in black marker.

Buzz smiled. "Being Andy's toy is the greatest mission of all. I wouldn't miss it for the universe."

DISNEY · PIXAR

TOY STORY AND BEYOND!

TOY CAMP

It's camp day!" Andy exclaimed as he rolled out of bed.

"Good morning, camper!" his mum called up the stairs. Andy was leaving for a week of sleepaway camp, where he would go hiking, swimming and maybe even fishing. He was really excited.

"Finish packing your clothes and come have breakfast!" called Andy's mum.

Andy filled his suitcase with shorts, shirts and pyjamas, plus a

swimsuit, sunscreen and bug spray. He latched the suitcase shut and looked around the room.

"Goodbye!" Andy said to his toys. "I'll be home soon." He picked up his suitcase and left the room.

As soon as Andy and his mother left for camp, the toys came to life. "I'm going to miss Andy," Woody the cowboy said.

"Me, too," said Hamm the piggy bank.

"Me, three," said Rex the dinosaur. "What will we do without Andy?"

"Well," said Woody, "we could play camp, too."

"That's a great idea!" Buzz Lightyear the space ranger cried.

"How do we play camp?" asked Hamm.

"That's easy," Woody replied. "We'll do everything indoors that Andy will do outdoors."

"What's the name of our camp, Woody?" Slinky Dog asked.

"How about . . . Camp Toy Chest?" said Woody.

"To Camp Toy Chest and beyond!" cried Buzz.

The Green Army Men marched out of the closet.

"I will be the camp captain," said Sarge. He walked over to Mr Mike. "Lights out!" he announced. "Everybody go to bed!"

"But it isn't bedtime," said Rex.

"Then let's put together tents," Sarge replied.

The toys looked around for something to use as tents.

A few minutes later, Buzz crawled out from under the bed carrying some of Andy's T-shirts. "Buzz Lightyear to Camp Toy Chest: I have found our tents!" called Buzz.

The toys helped each other pitch their tents, using pencils for poles.

"I'm too big for my tent," said Rex. As he tried to get out, he tripped over a tent pole.

So, Bo Peep found two kites and helped him make a tepee to sleep in.

"Thank you," said Rex.

"Time for bed," Sarge announced.

"It's bedtime?" Hamm asked. "Did the sun even go down?"

"No, silly," Bo Peep said. "I think Sarge is just having us practise so we're ready for the real thing. He must think this is boot camp, not fun camp."

Sarge overheard Bo Peep. Oh, *fun* camp, he thought. I can do that. "Never mind," he said. "Let's play tug-of-war instead."

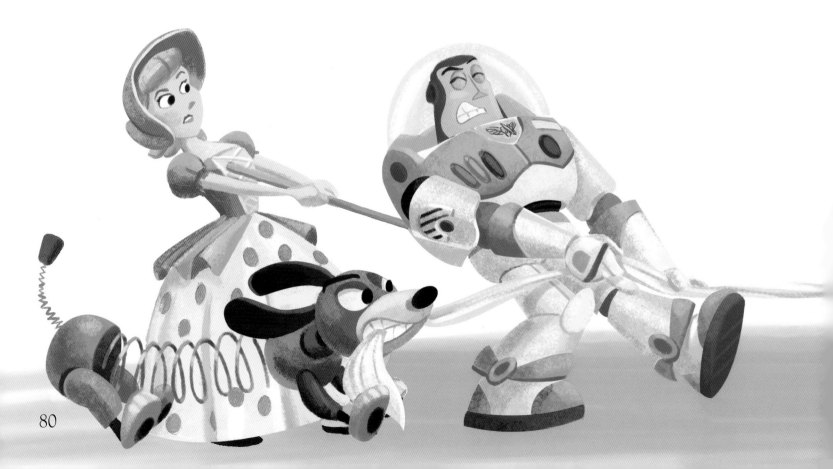

The toys cheered. They tied Andy's socks together to make a rope and played three rounds of tug-of-war. During the final game, Slinky Dog stretched himself as far as he could, backing up all the way to the wall.

On the other side, Rex held onto the rope tightly, but the socks finally slipped between his claws. The toys toppled over onto each other and Slinky Dog's team won.

Later that afternoon, Sarge ran over to Mr Mike and announced that it was time to play Capture the Flag.

Woody explained the rules of the game to the other toys. They made flagpoles out of markers. They put a small scrap of fabric on one pole and Bo Peep's bonnet on the other to make the flags.

When they started to play, Buzz pointed at something. Rex looked the other way, and Buzz sped by him and captured the flag!

"Huddle up, team," said Hamm. "We need a plan."

"I'll scare Buzz, then Woody can run past him and capture their flag,"

Rex suggested. His teammates looked doubtful. The dinosaur always tried to be scary, but he never really was. "I can do it!" Rex insisted.

So, the toys went back on the field. Rex ran over to Buzz and roared.

But Buzz didn't get scared. "Whoa, Rex," he said. "You got a frog in your throat?"

Rex frowned.

The toys played all afternoon. Everyone had lots of fun.

Soon, it started to get dark and the toys were tired. They decided to sit around a campfire.

The toys climbed to the top of Andy's dresser and got his battery-powered night-light. They set it on the floor, turned it on and sat around it.

"Now, let's tell scary stories!" Hamm cried.

Woody told a story about a really spooky haunted house. Everyone shivered. Next, Hamm told a story about the evil Dr Pork Chop. At the end, Bo Peep got so frightened, she let out a little scream. Then, it was Rex's turn. He told a story about the ghost of a stegosaurus. But the toys didn't get scared. They just yawned.

"All right, now it's finally time for lights out!" called Sarge. The toys went to their tents and fell asleep.

The next day, the toys needed something to do.
"How about we go for a hike?" asked Rex.
"Sure!" cried Woody. "Lead the way, Captain!"
Sarge and the other Green Army Men led the
toys through the maze of objects under Andy's bed.
They climbed up the leg of the bed and across the

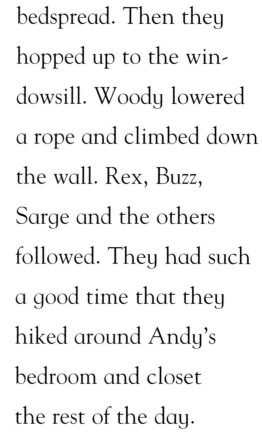

bedspread. Then they
hopped up to the win-
dowsill. Woody lowered
a rope and climbed down
the wall. Rex, Buzz,
Sarge and the others
followed. They had such
a good time that they
hiked around Andy's
bedroom and closet
the rest of the day.

All week long, the toys had fun playing camp.

The night before Andy was to come home, the toys decided to have a talent show. Buzz was the judge.

First, Bo Peep made her sheep disappear and reappear. Then, Woody showed off his rodeo skills as he jumped on RC Car and roped Hamm. Then, the Green Army Men did acrobatics.

Rex didn't have a talent, but he had an idea. During the show, he quietly got up and hid behind a bucket near the stage.

At the end of the show, Buzz stood up and cleared his throat. He was ready to announce the winner.

"And the winner is . . ." He paused.

Just then, Rex sprang from his hiding place and let out a mighty roar.

"*Aaaa!*" Buzz yelled. He was really frightened. He turned to run away and slipped. When he realized it was Rex who had roared, he grinned sheepishly and got up.

The other toys giggled. Rex beamed. He had finally scared someone!

Buzz turned to Rex and congratulated him. Then he gave Rex a ribbon for Best Act. The toys all clapped.

As he turned the lights off that night, Woody smiled. *I hope Andy had as much fun at his camp as we did at ours,* he thought.

The next morning, before Andy came home, the toys cleaned and straightened up his room. They folded his T-shirts and put them away. They put the pens and pencils back in his pencil case, and they arranged themselves neatly around the room.

Soon, Andy raced up the stairs. "Hi, every-one!" he cried. "I had so much fun at camp, but I missed all of you!"

We missed you, too, Andy, Woody thought. Welcome home.

90

TO INFINITY AND BEYOND!

One bright and sunny Saturday afternoon, Andy was playing outside. His toys were all in his room, looking for something to do.

Then Buzz Lightyear thought up the perfect activity – a launching-pad contest! He split the toys up into teams.

Each team had to design their own launching pad. The team with the most exciting launch would be the winner.

The teams worked for a little while, then Buzz got their attention. "Planning phase complete," he announced. "It's time to see which team did the best. When I say 'blast off', you should rocket your subject across Andy's room and into the pile of pillows at the other end!"

"Let's begin with team number one," said Buzz. "Three . . . two . . . one . . . blast off!" he shouted.

Using Slinky Dog as a slingshot, Rex and Bo Peep launched Woody into the air and clear across the room.

"Yee-hah!" Woody shouted as he soared over the other toys and landed on the pile of pillows.

"Ooooooh," said one Little Green Alien, amazed.

"A mystic launch," said another Little Green Alien.

"Aaaaaah," said the third Little Green Alien.

"Team number two," said Buzz, "you're next. Three . . . two . . . one . . . blast off!"

On Buzz's signal, a unit of Green Army Men used one of Andy's T-shirts like a trampoline. They began to bounce Jessie up and down. One, two, three – each bounce was higher than the one before.

The fourth time, the Green Army Men tilted the shirt and bounced Jessie right across the room.

"Yeeeee-haaaah!" she yelled out as she was launched into the air.

"Ooooooh," said one Little Green Alien.

"Unearthly distance," said another Little Green Alien.

"Aaaaaah," said the third Little Green Alien.

"Team number three, are you ready?" Buzz asked. They nodded. "Three . . . two . . . one . . . blast off!" Buzz shouted.

And with that, Hamm and Bullseye jumped off Andy's dresser and down onto the launching pad.

Their weight shot Robot across the room, towards the pillows. "Ooooooh," said one Little Green Alien.

"A rocket of power," said another Little Green Alien.

"Aaaaaah," said the third Little Green Alien.

97

"Okay, my turn!" exclaimed Buzz. He got on RC Car. "Three . . . two . . . one . . . blast off!" Buzz rolled down the bedspread and sped onto a nearby race-car track.

At the end, the track turned upwards, launching Buzz and the car high into the air.

"To infinity and beyond!" Buzz shouted as he aimed for the pile of pillows.

"Ooooooh," said one Little Green Alien.

"Cosmic momentum," said another Little Green Alien.

But the third Little Green Alien didn't say anything. He was nowhere to be found.

Just then – *squeak, squeak, squeak* – a little noise came from inside a jack-in-the-box.

Working together, two Little Green Aliens turned the toy onto one side and opened the lid. When they did, the spring within it was released and . . .

"Aaaaaah!" said the third Little Green Alien, as he took flight and soared towards the pillows. The toys all cheered. The Little Green Aliens were the winners! What a fun afternoon it had been.

A Tight Squeeze

"Calling all toys, calling all toys," Woody the cowboy announced. "The coast is clear."

It was early one morning, and Andy had just left for school. Since he would be gone all day, the toys had the room to themselves. They were ready to have some fun.

"So, Woody," Rex the dinosaur said as the toys gathered in the centre of the floor, "what's this game you were telling us about?"

Woody smiled. "It's called 'sardines'," he replied. "It's like hide-and-seek, except the toy who's 'It' is the one who hides, and everyone else tries to find him or her."

Buzz Lightyear the space ranger scratched his head. "I'm not sure I understand," he said. "What do you do when you find the hider?"

"Yeah, what do you do next?" asked Slinky Dog.

"Well," said Woody, "that's the fun part. When you find the hider, you hide with them and wait for someone else to find you both. Then, the next toy to find you hides with you, too, and so on, and so on. Get it?"

Most of the toys smiled and nodded at Woody. Bo Peep giggled. "Ooh, this is going to be fun!" she cried.

But Jessie the cowgirl was still confused about one thing. "So, by the end of the game, everyone is hiding together in one spot?" she asked.

Woody nodded. "Right," he said, "except for the last toy, who is still looking for the hiders. In the next game, that toy is 'It' – the one who hides!"

Now all the toys understood the rules and were ready to play!

"So let's decide who's 'It'," Woody suggested. "I'm thinking of a number between one and one hundred. Whoever guesses closest to that number is 'It'."

The toys took turns guessing. Woody was thinking of forty-nine. Hamm the piggy bank guessed forty-seven. He was the closest, so he was 'It'.

"Okay, everybody," Woody announced. "Close your eyes and count to twenty-five while Hamm hides."

The toys covered their eyes and began to count aloud, "One . . . two . . . three . . ."

Meanwhile, Hamm hurried away and started to look for a good hiding place. "Hmm . . ." he said to himself as he considered hiding inside Andy's toy chest. "Nah, too obvious. That's the first place they'd look."

"Ten . . . eleven . . . twelve . . ." the toys continued counting.

Hamm hurried over to Andy's bed and peeked under the cover. It was dark and dusty under the bed.

"Nah," said Hamm. "Too scary. I'm not hiding under there all by myself."

"Eighteen . . . nineteen . . . twenty . . ." the toys counted off.

Hamm was running out of time! With only seconds to spare, he spotted one of Andy's old lunchboxes, raced over to it, hopped inside, and closed the lid.

"Phew!" he whispered to himself. "That was close, but I'm hidden!" Only then did Hamm realize that it was even darker inside the closed lunchbox than it was under Andy's bed. "Huh," he said, feeling slightly panicked but trying to keep his cool. "I, uh, wonder how long it'll take for someone to find me."

The next toy to open the lunchbox lid was Woody, whose eyes lit up when he saw Hamm inside. He glanced over his shoulder to make sure he wasn't being watched before he hopped inside the lunchbox.

Soon, the lid opened and Jessie peeked in. "Yippee!" she cried. "Found ya, didn't I?"

But there wasn't much space left, so she got wedged between Hamm and Woody.

"Well, gosh, boys," said Jessie. "It's a little bit crowded in here, isn't it?"

A minute later, the lunchbox lid was lifted open and a Green Army Man peeked in. Upon spotting the toys, he waved to his battalion. "Target located. Move, move, move!" he ordered. The Green Army Men scaled the outside of the lunchbox and abseiled down the inside.

Within seconds, they were all in and the lid was closed again.

Woody started to feel a little cramped. "Uh, Hamm," he said, "could you scooch over a little?"

"Gee, Woody," Hamm replied, "I'd like to help you out, but I'm already squished up against the sergeant here." He pointed to the Green Army Man on the other side of him.

"Hmm . . ." said Woody. "This may become a problem."

The situation got worse as more and more toys found the hiders. Slinky Dog only managed to fit inside by standing over a Green Army Man.

"Ow, your paw is in my ear," the Green Army Man told Slinky Dog.

"Sorry, there's nowhere else for me to put it," Slinky Dog said.

Buzz heard the toys complaining and located the hiding place. "Make way, folks!" he exclaimed as he piled in. But as hard as he tried, he couldn't get the lid to close.

By the time Rex found the hiders, the lunchbox was completely full.

"Hey, no fair!" Rex exclaimed. "I found you guys, but there's no room for me to hide with you. What do I do now, Woody?"

"Shhhh!" Woody said, raising a finger to his lips. "Keep your voice down or everyone will come over and see where we're hiding."

But it was too late. The rest of the toys were already hurrying towards the overstuffed lunchbox.

"Oh, well," said Woody with a laugh. "They've found us, so this game is over. Everybody out!"

One by one, the toys tumbled out of the lunchbox and gathered around Hamm.

"Gosh, Hamm, couldn't you have picked a bigger hiding place?" Rex asked.

Hamm replied, "Well, yeah, but isn't the point of the game to get squished? Like sardines in a can? The game is called 'sardines', isn't it?"

The toys thought that over and had to agree. From then on, every time the toys played 'sardines' the hider made sure to pick a small hiding place – just to keep things interesting!

Ride 'Em Cowboy

"**Cowboy Bob** rode the bull for eight seconds", Andy read to his toys. "Cowboy Bob won the Silver Buckle. He was the rodeo champ!"

"Andy!" called his mum. "Into the car, or we'll be late for the rodeo."

114

"Yee-haw!"
yelled Andy, and he
raced from the room.

A **rodeo**...
thought Woody. Why not?

115

"Rodeo time!" yelled Woody. "Yahoo!" cried Jessie. "I'm the fastest rope in the West!"

"Oh, right," said Woody. "Let me show you how to rope a wild bronco."

"You mean a wild Bronco-saurus,"
said Hamm.

Rex grinned. "Who, me?"

"Watch this!" hollered Jessie.

"Triple play!" Jessie grinned. "Got the whole flock."

"Lucky ropin', cowgirl," said Woody. "But I'm the rodeo champ around these parts."

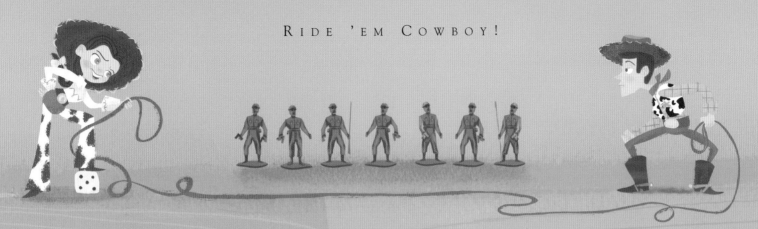

"Well, now . . ." said Jessie. "Care to pit your skills against mine, cowboy?"
"You're on!" said Woody.

"Aw right!" cried Slinky
Dog. "We're havin' a rodeo!"
"Let's get organized!"
called Buzz.

"Rodeo ring right here."
Buzz pointed. "Chute over there."
"I want to be in the rodeo!" said Rex.
"Ready!" announced Buzz. "First
event – steer wrestling!"
"I'll be a steer!"
called Rex.
"We've got it
covered, Rex," said
Buzz. "Hamm?"
"On it!" said
Hamm.

120

"Uh . . . how 'bout a practise run?" said Woody. "Don't worry, Woody," coached Slinky Dog. "Just take him down fast."

"Go!" called Buzz. "Yee-haw!" cried Woody as he and Bullseye burst out of the chute. "Moooo!" said Hamm. "I say, moo!" He jumped on a skate.

122

123

Hamm sped away from Woody. He hit a log and it went flying.

"Look out, Woody!" yelled Slinky.

"Bullseye – jump!" cried Woody.

Bullseye leaped over the log and galloped closer to the 'steer'.

Woody sprang off his horse and onto Hamm. He tried to wrestle him to the ground.

"Give it up, Woody," said Hamm. "I'm packin' twelve-fifty in quarters."

"Uhhhh," Woody groaned.

Next it was Jessie's turn. She whistled for Bullseye and jumped on his back. "Yee-haw!" she cried, galloping after the steer.

"What, again?" cried Hamm, and he took off running.

Bullseye caught up with Hamm.

Jessie jumped onto Hamm's back. She held on to his coin slot with one hand and tickled his belly with the other. **"Kitchy-kitchy-koo!"** she cried.

"Hoo-hoo-hah!" Hamm laughed. He rolled onto his side. **"Hoo-hoo! That tickles!"**

Jessie quickly tied up Hamm. Hamm stopped laughing. "**Hey!** No one told me about this part of the deal."

"I'm so glad I wasn't the steer!" said Rex.

128

"Nice wrestlin', little lady," said Buzz.

"What do you say now, Woody?" asked Jessie.

"Aw, I wasn't warmed up yet," said Woody.

"For cryin' out loud, **untie me!**" squealed Hamm.

129

"Barrel racing's next!"
said Buzz. **"Barrels?"**
The Little Green Aliens lined up.
"Jessie? You're first," called Buzz. "Go!"
Jessie rode into the ring. She guided Bullseye around the barrels and back again without knocking any of them over.
"Fourteen seconds!" cried Buzz.

"Beat that, cowboy," said Jessie.
"Watch me, cowgirl," said Woody as
he mounted his horse.
"Not too fast, Woody," warned Slinky.

"Go!" called Buzz.

"Ride like the wind, Bullseye!"
cried Woody.
Bullseye galloped for the barrels.

133

"Faster, Bullseye!"
shouted Woody. "We have to win!"
Bullseye galloped faster.

"Oooooooh!"
The aliens hunkered
down and shut
their eyes.

134

But Bullseye whizzed past them
and galloped out of the door.

"Aw, great!" said Slinky Dog.
"Just great!"

"The winner is **Jessie!**"
announced Buzz.

"Yay!" cheered the toys.

"Thanks a lot, Bullseye,"
muttered Woody.

135

"Last event – bull riding!" said Buzz. "Sarge? Call the bull!"
"Sir! Yes, sir!" said Sarge. He whistled.
Buster nosed open the door and ran into Andy's room.
"Bull reporting for duty, sir!" Sarge added.

"Think you can ride that bull for eight seconds, cowboy?" asked Jessie.
"Nothin' to it, cowgirl," said Woody.

"Rex?" called Buzz. "You want to be the rodeo clown?"

"Yes! Absolutely!" cried Rex. "But – how do I make balloon animals with my little arms?"

"No balloons," said Buzz. "If Woody gets thrown, your job is to keep the bull busy till he gets up."

"Don't worry, Rex," said Woody. "I'm not getting thrown!"

137

Woody climbed onto
Buster's back.
"Hey, finger paints!"
said Rex. "I'll make
myself a clown suit!"
"Rex, shhhhh!" said
Buzz. **"Woody? Go!"**

Buster jumped out of the chute and ran around the ring.

"Ride 'em, cowboy!" yelled Slinky.

"Hey, Jessie!" cried Woody.

"Watch this!"

And he stood up on
  Buster's back.

"Sit down, Woody!"
cried Slinky.
  Woody began
to wobble.

139

"Ahhhhhhh!"
Woody cried as he flew off
Buster's back.
**"To infinity and
beyond!"** called Buzz.

SPLAT!

Woody hit the wall and slid down.

Slinky Dog ran over. "You okay, Woody?"

"Yeahhhhh," said Woody.

"Next rider!" called Buzz.
"Yeeeeee-haaaaa!"
yelled Jessie.

She held tight as
Buster bucked and
kicked and raced
around Andy's room.

"Eight seconds
are up!" said Buzz.
"We have our
rodeo champ!"

8 SEC.

142

"**For a prize?**" said Buzz.
"I'd – uh – like you to have my Star
Command belt buckle."

"Thanks a heap, spaceman!"
exclaimed Jessie.

Buzz grinned. "Etch?" he called.
"Get blazin' for the closing campfire!"

143

Woody caught up with Jessie on her way to the campfire.

"Well, you beat me fair and square, cowgirl," he said.

"This time, cowboy," said Jessie. "But there's always next time."

Woody sat down – very slowly.
"Where does it hurt?" asked Jessie.
"Everywhere," said Woody.

"To the tune of 'Home on the Range'!" cried Buzz. **"Sing it!"**

All the toys sang:

If you've got a rope,
And a heart full of hope,
And a horse that won't gallop away!
Get some boots and a hat,
If you've got all of that,
Then you'll be a cowpoke someday!

"Listen," said Buzz as the song ended. "Footsteps!"

"Andy's home!" called Woody. "Places!"

Seconds later, Andy galloped into his room.
He grabbed Woody and Jessie. **"Rodeo time!"**
he cried. "Which one of you is gonna be the rodeo
champ?"

148

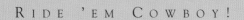

RIDE 'EM COWBOY!

You know, it doesn't matter who's champ, thought Woody. It's all about having fun with the other cowpokes. **Yee-haw!**

149

RODEO: A contest in which cowboys and cowgirls show how good they are at taking care of cattle. If a calf on a ranch gets sick, a cowboy or cowgirl has to rope it, tie it down, and hold it still so the vet can examine it. In a rodeo, these skills are shown off in the tie-down roping event.

Other exciting rodeo events are:

STEER WRESTLING or BULLDOGGING:
A steer is a male cow with long, sharp horns. In steer wrestling, a cowboy jumps off his horse onto a steer. He grabs it by the horns and 'wrestles' it to the ground. The cowboy who does this the fastest is the winner. A winning time might be three or four seconds.

BARREL RACING: This event is all about co-operation between a horse and a rider, often a cowgirl. Three barrels are set up in a line. A rider gallops into the ring, rides around each barrel in a cloverleaf pattern and then gallops out of the ring. The fastest rider is the winner. For every barrel a rider knocks over, five seconds are added to the time. A winning time can be thirteen or fourteen seconds.

BULL RIDING: This is the most dangerous event of all. Cowboys ride fully grown, two-thousand-pound bulls. To begin, the cowboy sits on a bull's back inside a chute. When the cowboy is ready, he nods and the gate goes up. The bull bursts out of the chute trying to buck the cowboy off his back. The cowboy holds on to a braided rope with one hand. If he touches the bull with his other hand, he loses. Riders try to stay on the bull's back for eight seconds.

THE END

Also available in the series...

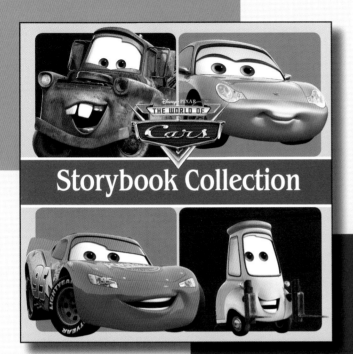

Storybook Collection

Storybook Collection

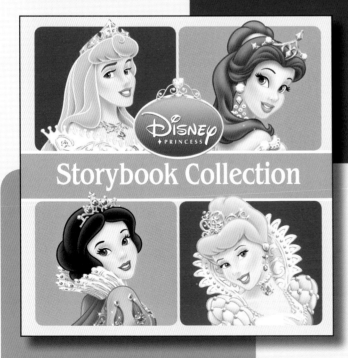

Storybook Collection

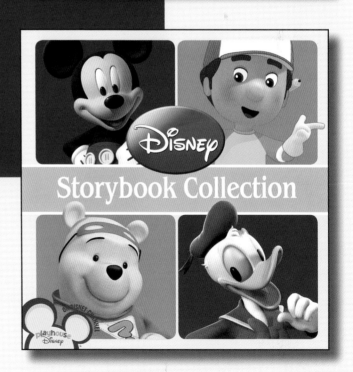

Storybook Collection